DO NOT REMOVE
CARDS FROM POCKET

That Terrible Baby

by **Jennifer Armstrong**

pictures by **Susan Meddaugh**

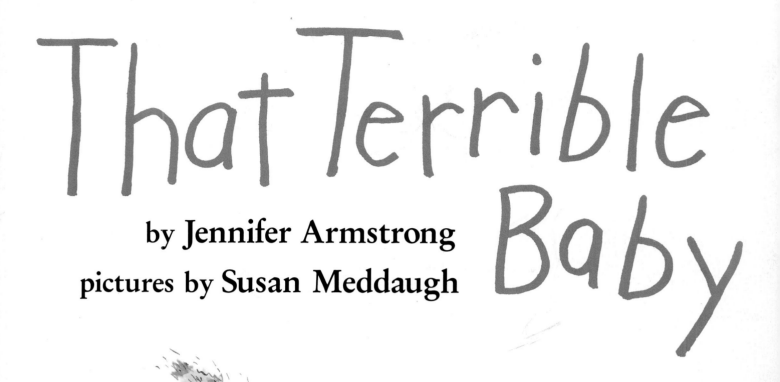

 TAMBOURINE BOOKS · NEW YORK

Text copyright © 1994 by Jennifer M. Armstrong
Illustrations copyright © 1994 by Susan Meddaugh

Inquiries should be addressed to Tambourine Books,
a division of William Morrow & Company, Inc.,
1350 Avenue of the Americas, New York, New York 10019.
The illustrations were prepared using watercolor and colored pencils.
Printed in Hong Kong by South China Printing Company (1988) Ltd.

Library of Congress Cataloging in Publication Data

Armstrong, Jennifer, 1961-   That terrible baby/by Jennifer M.
Armstrong; pictures by Susan Meddaugh.—1st ed.   p. cm.
Summary: Mom blames Eleanor and Mark for making a mess of the
house until she finally sees that the real culprit is the baby.
[1. Babies—Fiction.   2. Brothers and sisters—Fiction.
3. Behavior—Fiction.]   I. Meddaugh, Susan, ill.   II. Title.
PZ7.A73367Th 1994   [E]—dc20   93-14727 CIP AC
ISBN 0-688-11832-1.—ISBN 0-688-11833-X (lib. bdg.)
1 3 5 7 9 10 8 6 4 2
FIRST EDITION

This book is dedicated with great affection
to La Bella Della, a funny little kid.
Don't take it personally.
J.M.A.

For Sam and Win.
S.M.

Eleanor and Mark were worried.
There was a terrible baby in the house.

This terrible baby could crawl. It crawled through Mark's room and chewed up the eye patch of his pirate costume. It crawled across Dogbiscuit and made her yowl.

It crawled into Eleanor's room and ripped the gorilla poster off the wall. And it kept on crawling.

"Stop that baby!" Mark said.

Eleanor and Mark raced into the dining room. The terrible baby pulled down the tablecloth, and Mark's five-story card house cascaded to the floor. The terrible baby laughed and scrunched up the three of clubs and two of diamonds.

"Oh, no you don't!" Mark said, taking away the cards.

The terrible baby began to howl. Eleanor did her monkey act to make the baby stop.

When Mom came in, the terrible baby waved its arms and cooed like a dove.

"What's going on here?" Mom asked. "What a mess!"

"It was the baby," Mark explained.

Mom pointed to the smile on the baby's face.
"That is a perfect angel. Don't blame the baby. And pick up your cards, Captain."

Mark picked up the bent cards and grumbled about getting back to his ship, while the terrible baby crawled away.

"That baby is going to walk the plank!" Mark said.

The terrible baby crawled into the living room and
tossed all the magazines and coasters off the table.

Then the terrible baby crawled into the bathroom and put all the towels in the tub and turned the hot water on.

"Stop that baby!" Mark warned.

Eleanor turned the faucet off, and the baby howled.
Mark tried yodeling to make the baby laugh.
The baby howled even more.

"Why are you yelling at the baby?" Mom asked. She came in and saw the puddles on the floor. "What's this mess?"

"It was the baby, Mom," Eleanor explained.

"Don't be ridiculous," Mom said. "Now how about mopping up this water? And don't forget to shut the bathroom door!"

When Eleanor, Mark, and the terrible baby were alone again, the baby crawled away.

"I'm putting that baby in the zoo!" Eleanor said.

The terrible baby crawled into the kitchen and tipped over the cat food bowl and knocked over the garbage can.

Just as the terrible baby was about to eat a banana peel, Eleanor snatched it away. The baby howled.

"This is the last straw!" Mom said, running into the kitchen. "This place is a disaster. And don't blame it on the baby!"

"But Mom!" Mark began.

Mom picked up the baby. "You two clean up this mess and then sit at the kitchen table and don't even move."

The terrible baby smiled as Mom took it away.

Eleanor and Mark cleaned up the kitchen, and then sat and sulked.

Dogbiscuit hurried by.

Then the baby crawled in after her again, all clean and shiny. Dogbiscuit bolted out the cat door. The baby put on speed.

"Mom?" Eleanor called as the cat disappeared. "Can I move?"

"No!" Mom called back.

The terrible baby poked its head through the flap.

"Mom!" Mark called. "Can I get up?"
"NO!" Mom called back.

The terrible baby squeezed halfway through the opening.

"That baby ate my eye patch," Mark said.
"That baby ripped down my gorilla poster," Eleanor said.
The terrible baby disappeared.
"LOOK OUT!"

Mark and Eleanor jumped up and yanked the door open.
Just as the terrible baby was about to fall down the steps,
Eleanor scooped it up.

The baby looked up with a happy gurgle.
"That was close," Eleanor said.
"It's not such a terrible baby, really," Mark said.

Mom came out onto the porch. "Hey, why are you out here?" she asked.

"It was the baby," Mark explained.

"For the last time—"

The baby crawled back through the cat door and disappeared. Mom scratched her head.

"That's one speedy crawler," she admitted. "I'd better go in."

Mark looked at Eleanor.
Eleanor looked at Mark.
"OK," they said. "But we'll stay out here."